WRONGLY ACCUSED

ANTONIO (FUDGE) FORD

Copyright © 2024 Antonio (Fudge) Ford
All rights reserved.

Dedication

Tribute to Daisy and Lee Ford, Moma Ruby and Grandpa James Leblue, Kenneth Leblue (the father), LIL Lee Ford, Tracy Lerone Leblue and Brandon Leblue (the brothers); the Williams family of Bastrop, Tx.

Acknowledgment

My shout-out goes to Aurora County jail processing for letting me keep my notes when I first started this book. If you had made me throw my papers away, this book would've never made it.

To my mother, Cynthia Ford, Michael Collins, Kareem Evans, Paulette Munnerlyn, Mildred Mazyck, Joyce Owens, Joseph (Juice100) Johnson, Darrell Davis, Jeanette Harris, Shandrea Bowie, and G. Cordova, thank you for opening up your home when I didn't have anywhere to go!

To my editor, Faith Loveth, you are the best! This was my first book, and she walked me through the whole process. Thank you for being patient and understanding.

I want to acknowledge the community in which I was raised in Compton, CA. (Mob) and Lynwood, CA. (Cross Atlantic). May peace be with the streets.

Additionally, I thank Danita Higsby for typing out some pages (I know she thought I was going to leave her out!). Finally, to the love of my life, Princess Ford, you never kept a secret and always stayed real.

ONE

"DAMN! TIME FOR WORK already," Terrell said as he reached for his alarm and pressed the off button. "Oh yea, let me call Dee and see if he wants to role with me over at my baby mom's house so I can introduce him to Sheila, her little sister." He grabbed the phone and dialed 5551212.

"Hello," Dee said.

"What's Up, Man? Time to wake up!" Terrell replied.

"What you talking 'bout? We still have two hours!" Dee retorted.

"Nooooo! Remember I was going to introduce you to Kelly's little sister, Danna?" Terrell said.

"Oh yea!" Dee replied.

"So, get ready and meet me at the bus stop in 30 minutes. That way, we can kick it over there for a second before heading to work," Terrell told Dee.

"Okay. Bet!" Dee replied.

"Gone!" Terrell said.

◆◆◆◆◆

At the same time, across town, Bad News is up early, smoking a blunt, pacing the floor. "Damn, why ain't this nigga answering the phone?!" He said to himself, referring to his childhood friend, Trouble. All of a sudden, Trouble picked up the phone.

"Damn, nigga why you not answering the phone? You know it's time to get that money. Where you at? Did you get the G-Ride?" Bad News asked.

"Yea, nigga. I'm on my way! Be there in about 20 minutes. What about you? You got the heats?" Trouble asked.

"Don't ask me no shit like that. Just hurry yo ass up!" Bad News snapped.

After a few minutes, Trouble called Bad News. "I'm outside," Trouble said. A few moments later, a 6'4," 240-pound muscular, built, heavily-tatted guy named Bad News walked out. Bad News hopped into the van that Trouble had stolen the previous night.

"Look, man, I've been buying coke from this mutha fucka, Oscar, for two years, and this mutha fucka can't even front me a funky-ass nine-piece! Fuck him! Now I'm gone take it ALL! I been watching him for two weeks now. He drops his wife and daughter off at 8:00 am, and he'll be back by 8:45 am. We will pull up in the back, and I'll pick the lock and will surprise his bitch ass!" Bad News ranted. "Now, look Trouble, don't bitch up when we get in here, man. If this mother fucker blinks wrong, kill him!"

"Fa Sho! Aye, but if it goes well, we gon' let him live, right?" Trouble replied.

"Yea, whatever nigga," Bad News replied.

♦♦♦♦♦

Terrell and Dee arrived at Kelly's house and knocked twice on the door.

"Who is it?" Kelly asked from behind the door. Terrell:

"You know who it is. Stop playing and open the door," Terrell replied.

"Hold on, let me throw something on," Kelly replied. After a few seconds, the door opened, and there stood a thick, chocolate-sexy black woman with just a robe and a scarf around her thick, freshly pressed hair. "Why you here so early?" she looked to the left at Dee, then added, "And who is this? You didn't tell me you were bringing somebody with you."

"My bad, you know I have to work today. I told Dana that I would introduce her to my coworker Dee. And by the way, Dee, this is my baby momma/fiancé, Kelly," Terrell introduced.

"Hi," Dee greeted.

"Hi. Go ahead and have a seat," Kelly replied sweetly, then called out, "Dana!"

"What?" a voice replied.

"Come out here and meet Terrell's friend," Kelly yelled.

"Here I come!" Dana replied.

"Where's my little man?" Terrell asked.

"He's in the room watching cartoons," Kelly replied. As Kelly finished her last statement, Dana walked out; she was almost a spitting image of Kelly, except she was a little taller and had a slightly bigger ass.

Dee stared in awe.

"Dee, this is Dana. Why don't y'all chop it? I'mma go in the room with my son," Terrell told Dee.

"Bet!" Dee replied.

Dana sat down next to Dee on the couch, and they started talking. After five minutes, Kelly walked into the living room with Terrell Jr.

"Dana, watch JR for a sec. I'm trynna get my freak on real quick," Kelly told Dana, and with a wink, she disappeared into the bedroom and shut the door behind her.

3

"Y'all nasty! That's how you got this one. Don't make any more! I can't be watching two badass kids!" Dana yelled after Kelly.

◆◆◆◆◆

Bad News and Trouble pulled up slowly and parked in front of a building.

"Right here. He's there. He must have took them early. Go pick the lock on the side door and come back," Bad News instructed Trouble.

"Yep!" Trouble replied.

After five minutes, Trouble returned.

"Did you get it? Did anybody see you?" Bad News asked anxiously.

"Naw, man! You know burglary is my specialty!" Trouble replied.

The two put their gloves on and cocked their loaded nine-millimeter guns, put them in their waist, then slid on their stocking caps on their heads before hopping out of the van, both carrying tools as if they were called to fix something.

"Act normal!" Bad News told Trouble.

They both headed to the side door, and Bad News took a peek through the side window. Oscar was in the living room watching videos while talking on the phone and smoking. Bad News then gave Trouble the signal to go ahead, and Trouble turned the doorknob as slow and carefully as he could, and both men sneaked in, pulling their stocking caps over their faces just before they entered the house.

In a flash, both men were in the living room, their guns drawn, yelling, "Don't move! Don't move! Get ya face down, mutherfucka! Make a move, and I'll blow your fuckin' head off! Where the shit at?!"

Oscar was so surprised that he threw his hands up, screaming, "Wait, wait, what are you talking about?"

"You know what I'm talking about! Turn around and put your hands behind your back," Bad News retorted. He whipped some duct tape out of his bag and wrapped Oscar's hands up. Then he turned to Trouble and said, "Tear this muthafucka up and make sure ain't nobody else in here!"

Trouble immediately started searching the house for goods.

"Look, don't make me ask you again! I want the drugs and the money! You got FIVE seconds, and I'mma blow your fuckin' head off!" Bad News said. Holding the gun to Oscar's head, he started counting. "One, two, three, four…"

"Okay, Okay! In the kitchen, up under the stove," Oscar screamed.

"Go check it out," Bad News told Trouble.

Trouble went into the kitchen, moved the stove, and discovered a hole in the floor with a bag in it. Trouble opened the bag, and bingo, he yelled, "6 bricks and eight bundles of cash!" Trouble ran back into the living room. "Let's go, I got it!" he said, holding up the bag.

Oscar was still pleading for his life. "Don't kill me, man. I have a daughter and a wife. You got what you wanted, so just go!"

Bad News ordered Oscar to turn around, with the gun still pointed at his head.

"I've got good news and bad news," Bad News started one of his favorite sayings. "Which one do you want first?" Bad News then pulled up his mask, and Oscar's mouth dropped. "I'mma give you the bad news first…"

"Nooooo!" Oscar screamed.

BANG! The shot to the head drowned out Oscar's screams. BANG! BANG! BANG! Three more shots to the body, and Oscar lay dead as a doornail.

"Damn Nigga!" Trouble yelled. "Why you kill him!?!"

"Stop acting like a bitch! Sometimes I wonder about you, Trouble! Boy, if yo momma didn't raise me when momma died, I'd kill you too! C'mon, let's walk out the front door," Bad News rebuked. "ACT NORMAL! You can do that, can't you?"

What Trouble didn't know was that the caller who was on the phone with Oscar never hung up and was listening the whole time. So, right as Trouble and Bad News pulled off, the police pulled up.

♦♦♦♦♦

Two houses down, Dee and Dana hit it off really well when Dee realized what the time was.

"Damn, this nigga 'bout to make us late for work!" Dee said. He walked over to the bedroom door and knocked. "Yo nigga, we got 15 minutes to make it to the bus stop. Hurry up! If I'm late one more time, I'm gon' get fired!"

Terrell yelled through the door. "Alright, give me five more minutes. We'll make it."

Dee sat back down next to Dana and finished choppin' it up. Five minutes went by, and then Dee knocked on the door again. Actually, it was more of a bang this time.

"C'mon man, I can't be late! I'm out!" Dee yelled through the door.

"Okay, nigga hold up!" Terrell yelled.

Dee exchanged numbers with Dana and headed to the door. The bedroom door flew open, and Terrell ran out, putting his shirt on and grabbing his backpack. Kelly was right behind him, her hair all matted. She had a slight look of exhaustion on her face.

"Hold up, Dee!" Terrell yelled, then turned and kissed Kelly, kissed his son on the forehead, told them both he loved them, and he and Dee ran to the bus stop.

While in transit to the bus stop, Trouble and Bad News crossed paths with Terrell and Dee. They all stared each other down. Bad News slowly reached under his shirt. Trouble quickly grabbed his hand and whispered, "Naw."

Dee and Terrell resumed running in hopes of catching their bus. "Scuse me. Scuse me. Look out," the two kept saying, weaving in and out of people in passing.

"Oh shit!" Dee said when he knocked an old lady's trash out of her hand as she was dumping it in the outside trash can. He stopped and picked it up. "Sorry, Madam."

"C'mon, the bus is pulling up!" Terrell yelled.

Barely making it to the bus stop, they both hop on, gasping for air. "We made it!" Dee said, flashing his bus pass and heading towards the back of the bus.

♦♦♦♦♦

Trouble and Bad News hopped in the stolen work van smoothly and undetected and rolled off just as smoothly as they had rolled up.

TWO

"911 DISPATCH LAURA SPEAKING. What's your emergency?" the operator asked.

"I think my uncle's been shot!" a panicked voice replied.

"Calm down, sir. What's your address?" the operator asked.

"No, no. Not *my* address! I was on the phone with my uncle when ... his address is 3685 Glencoe St, Denver, CO," the caller replied.

"Okay, sir, a unit is on its way," the operator assured.

In what seemed like seconds, a squad car pulled up to the address just given, and two officers approached the house. One went to the side while the other knocked on the front door. There was no response. The officer knocked again, but still, there was no response.

Just then, the officer on the side spotted Oscar lying on the floor in a puddle of blood through the side window. He then hurried up to the front door and alerted the other officer, and together, they kicked the front door in.

After quickly making sure the house was empty, one of the officers said, "We're too late! Call homicide."

In a few minutes, Homicide Detectives Ford and Smith pulled up to a taped-off crime scene in a dark blue unmarked car. Detective Smith was a longtime vet who was two years shy of retirement, a lifelong overweight functional alcoholic, with 74 solved murders under his belt. Detective Ford, on the other hand, has just been assigned to homicide, and this was only his second case.

They both hopped out of the car and approached the yellow tape. They walked inside the house, and Detective Smith asked one of the officers at the scene, "What we got here?"

"A 27-year-old Hispanic male named Oscar Velasquez. We found him laying herewith, one to the head and two to three to the body. Looks like a robbery," an officer replied.

"Any witnesses?" Detective Smith asked.

"Yes, we have two witnesses that say they seen two black males fleeing from the scene," the officer informed Detective Smith.

"Clear my murder scene so we can work our magic. Take the witnesses down to the station for questioning," Detective Smith said.

Detectives Smith and Ford swept the crime scene for prints and DNA, then headed to the station to question the witnesses.

After interviewing the witnesses, they learned that one of the suspects had knocked over a trash can and stopped to pick it up before fleeing the scene. Detective Ford then went back by the crime scene to dust the trash can for prints.

Detective Smith had a description of the suspects drawn and waited for the prints on the trash can to come back. Once the results were in, the prints matched a black male named Deondre Sanders, which also matched the sketch drawn from the witness's description.

"Man, they make our job easier and easier every crime," Detective Smith said out loud. "Ford, get this out to the press ASAP so we can wrap this up. Also, round up troops so we can check his last known address. This should be an open-and-shut case."

As the city of Colorado watched their regularly scheduled programs, they were suddenly interrupted by a breaking news message.

"A murder has occurred today on the 3600 block of Glencoe in Denver, Colorado. The assailants were two black males, one named Deondre Sanders. Here is a sketch of the other suspect. If you have any information leading to the arrest of these two men, please call the Crime Stoppers at 5527463. If you should see these two men, Please be cautious! They may be armed and are dangerous!" the news reporter announced.

Everybody, including Kelly, Bad News, and all Dee's family and friends who just saw the news flash simultaneously said, "What the hell?!"

However, everyone except Dee and Terrell, who are busy working unloading trucks at a noisy warehouse, saw the news flash. One of the rules at the job was that phones were not allowed on the warehouse floor. It was a quick way to get instantly terminated!

Kelly, in shock, called Terrell over and over again, but there was no answer. Dee's mother and uncle also called him after watching the news in disbelief.

A couple of coworkers who were on their break in the lunch room, watching the breaking news on television, called the number that was flashed on the screen after noting that their coworkers who had just been flashed on the screen were at work. They could not believe what they just saw.

Detectives Ford and Smith were notified, and within 15 minutes, they had the warehouse surrounded. The Swat team then moved in suddenly, yelling, "Freeze! Don't Move!"

Surprised, both men threw their hands in the air.

"Wait! Wait! There must be a mistake!" yelled Dee as they threw him into a squad car. Terrell thought that this was happening because he periodically took miscellaneous items from the warehouse, so he remained silent.

Once at the station, Terrell and Dee were separated for questioning. Detectives Smith and Ford discussed who would play "bad cop" this time and decided to question Dee first because he looked like he would crack the easiest. Then Detective Ford started the questioning.

"So, do you know what you are here for?" Detective Ford asked.

"NO! Why?" Dee replied.

"Look, you little black mutha fucka, we ain't got no time for games! You're busted! Now tell us, why did you kill Oscar Velasquez? Was it for drugs?" Detective Smith answered impatiently.

"What? I don't know what y'all are talking about! This definitely is a mistake! I want a lawyer! Where's my mom?" Dee said.

"Look, be cool; we have two eyewitnesses that can place you at the scene of the crime," Detective Ford told him.

"And your fingerprints, punks!" Detective Smith added.

"If these witnesses can point you out in a lineup, you're done!" Detective Ford said, leaning over Dee's shoulder. "Look, I'm on your side; just tell us what happened."

"I told you, man, nothing! You have the wrong people!" Dee replied.

"Okay. Have it your way!" Detective Smith said, walking out of the room and slamming the door.

"Look, Deondre, I'mma give you a little time to think. Here's some paper maybe you would rather write it down. I'll be back. Do you want a soda?" Detective Ford told Dee.

Dee put his head down without a word. Detective Ford walked out of the room. Then, both detectives meet in the hall to discuss the situation.

"He's tougher than I expected," Detective Smith said.

"I know. I almost believe him. Let's see what we can get out of Terrell," Detective Ford replied. They walked into the room where

Terrell was waiting, no longer looking like a tough black male but a scared lil boy who had no clue as to what was going on.

"I did it! It was just a PlayStation 3 and a TV. Y'all act like I killed somebody!" Terrell said as soon as the detectives walked in.

"Nice try, dumb ass! Don't try and play me. You know you are here for murder!" Detective Smith said.

"What? I ain't killed nobody! Now, I am even more confused," Terrell said. "This ain't about the stuff I took from the warehouse?" Terrell asked.

"No! Where were you at today, about 9:00 am?" Detective Smith asked.

"I was at my son's mom's house. I can prove it!" Terrell said.

"Okay," Detective Ford said.

"Bullshit! Y'all was robbing Oscar!" Detective Smith cut in.

"let's check his alibi," Detective Ford told Detective Smith calmly, and then they both walked out of the room.

"It's been a long day. Book them on a 48-hour hold, and we will get back to them tomorrow," Detective Smith said.

"Okay," Detective Ford replied.

◆◆◆◆◆

Trouble and Bad News parked their getaway van at a remote location and torched it. Now, at their hideout, which is a low-key spot in the Valley, they began counting the money when, all of a sudden, they saw the news flash.

They were both shocked.

"Wow, they think them ole schoolboy-looking ass niggas did that shit?!" Trouble said. "Hell yea!"

"I have an idea; let's go find a spot to throw the gun and then call the snitch line and give a tip," Bad News suggested.

"Hell yea! That's what I'm saying," Trouble agreed.

They walked to a nearby phone booth after discarding their guns and dialed the number from the TV screen.

"Hello, crime stoppers? ... Yes, I have information about a murder," Trouble said.

"Okay, go ahead," the voice from the other end urged.

"Well, I was on my way to work when I saw two men throw a gun in the bushes," Trouble informed.

"Okay, what's your name?" the operator asked.

"I would like to remain anonymous," Trouble replied.

"Okay," the operator said.

Trouble clicked the phone. "Aye, I think I know where these niggas was coming from," Trouble told his partner.

"Oh yea?" Bad News asked.

"Yea. Remember Kelly, who used to go to Kimble High and got a sister named Dana?" Trouble asked.

"Yea. Dark-skinned, short, with a big booty?" Bad News replied.

"Yea! She stay on that block, and if I'm not mistaken, that's her dude or baby daddy," Trouble told him.

"Yea, I think it's time we pay that bitch a visit for old time's sake," Bad News said.

The next morning, Trouble and Bad News sat in Trouble's 1988 Cutlass, waiting for Kelly or Dana to come out. Just as they guessed, Kelly and Terrell Jr came out with Terrell Jr dressed for daycare. As the duo approached Kelly's car, Trouble yelled Kelly's name. Kelly turned around to see who was calling her.

"It's me, Marcus Jones, from school," Trouble said.

As Kelly started to speak, Bad News put a gun to her waist through his coat so it was not visible. He did so discreetly so as not to alarm her son.

"Shut the fuck up, turn around, and walk back into the house," Bad News told her. Before she could second guess his order, Trouble picked up TJ and started walking towards the door. Kelly opened the door, and they followed behind her.

"Look, I don't have any money. Please don't hurt me or my son," Kelly told them.

"We're not here to hurt you; we just want to warn you when the police come questioning you. You make sure you say nothing, not a damn thing! If they ask if you seen your lil boyfriend the day they question you about it, I'mma need you to say no and stick to that! If not, I'mma kill you and your son! I also know your mom and dad still stay in that old house you grew up in, and your cousin who manages that dollar store. Don't make me go there!" Bad News warned.

Trouble put TJ down, and Kelly grabbed him in horror. As Bad News and Trouble walked out, Trouble looked back at Kelly, who was still frantic in tears and shaking, and told her, "Oh, and tell Dana I said Waddup!" The two men laughed and hopped in the car and rolled out.

◆◆◆◆◆

It was still early morning at the police station. Dee and Terrell were in two different cells. Dee woke up thinking this was all a big nightmare. He looked around at the cell, and reality sank in. "Yep, this is real," he muttered to himself.

In the other cell, Terrell paced the floor anxiously, waiting for some good news, knowing his baby momma would straighten this all out since he was at her house when this murder took place.

It was just another day for Detectives Smith and Ford as they crossed paths in the break room for their daily morning coffee and doughnuts.

"Top of the morning!" Detective Smith greeted.

"Hey, Smith," Detective Ford replied.

"Are you ready to close this case?" Detective Smith asked.

"I have been meaning to talk to you about something. I ran background checks on the suspects, and it's quite interesting. Sanders has no priors. He actually was a 3.0 student in high school, an all-American running back, and was headed to LSU for college in the fall on a full-ride scholarship! Jones only had one juvenile conviction for assault after beating his stepdad up for attacking his mother. Both men have been holding down a steady job. It just doesn't make any sense," Detective Ford replied.

"I tell you what don't make sense: you thinking the idiots didn't commit the crime when the proof is in the pudding! Do you know how many times I've seen kids with a bright future fuck up their lives? Look at all the facts! Now, c'mon, let's go check out their *alibi*," Detective Smith replied.

Detectives Smith and Ford pulled up at Dana's residence. Walking to the door, they noticed that the murder scene was just three houses down. They shared a look without words at that realization, then knocked.

"Who is it?" Dana asked. Detectives Smith and Ford announced themselves, and Dana opened the door. "Yes? May I help you?" she asked.

"Yes, we just have a couple of questions for you," Detective Ford told her.

Glancing over the Detective's shoulder, Dana saw Trouble's car passing by. He stared at her with a look of threat locked in his eyes.

"Look, I don't know nothing, okay?" Dana said.

"Ma'am, we haven't asked you anything yet," Detective Smith said.

"May we come in?" Detective Ford asked.

"Do you have a warrant?" Dana asked.

"Look, we're here trying to help your boyfriend, Terrell," Detective Ford told her.

"I haven't seen him in weeks, okay?" Dana said, slamming the door. Detectives Smith and Ford look at each other in disbelief. As the detectives walked back to their cars, both men commented on how odd that was, and they headed back to the station.

On the way to the station, Detective Ford told Detective Smith, "Something just isn't right! Did you see how nervous she was? It was almost like she was told not to talk to us. I don't know, Smith, it just doesn't add up."

Upon arriving at the station, Detective Smith ordered the suspects back to the interrogation room. But before they joined them in the interrogation room, Detectives Smith and Ford had a brief meeting at their desk.

"Well, we have witnesses who can place them at the scene and a murder weapon. Also, their alibi didn't check out, plus there is a motive," Detective Smith said.

"What's that?" Detective Ford asked.

"Hell, he was watching Oscar selling drugs from his baby mama's house and decided to rob him. Plain and simple. Case closed! That right there is enough to charge them. We did our job; we just have to let a grand jury decide if they are guilty or not," Detective Smith replied.

"Okay, but I still have doubts about this one, Smith. Let's see if we can get a confession," Detective Ford insisted.

The detectives then walked into the room where Terrell was waiting.

"Well, your alibi didn't check out, son," Detective Smith told Terrell.

"What? I don't get it!" Terrell said, anxious.

"Now you need to be a man and fess up," Detective Smith told him.

"Fuck you, pig! I didn't kill nobody! I'm getting a lawyer!" Terrell yelled, frustrated.

"Have it your way," Detective Smith told him. He opened the door and called for an officer. "Officer, book Mister Jones under robbery and first-degree murder," he instructed.

Both detectives walked out the door and into the interrogation room Dee was in.

"Well, it's not looking good for you, son," Detective Ford informed Dee.

"What do you mean?" Dee asked.

"Your alibi didn't check out," Detective Ford told him.

"So, what does that mean?" Dee asked.

"All the evidence points to you and Terrell. Look, kid, I ran a background check on you, and I know you're not the type of kid that will do something like that. So, if your friend Terrell set this whole thing up and convinced you to do it, just let us know," Dee told him.

"You have a bright future. Don't go down with this idiot," Detective Smith added.

"Look, man, I'm telling the truth. I didn't do nothing," Dee said.

"D, I'm trying to help you, and you're not telling us nothing," Detective Ford said.

"Wait a minute; I seen two guys walking to a van," Dee said, a light bulb going off in his head.

"That's good and dandy, but you have nobody to back you up. Plus, everybody pointed you out. Last chance," Detective Smith said.

"I didn't do shit!" Dee yelled, frustrated.

"Tell it to the judge," Detective Smith said. "Officer, book him!"

♦♦♦♦♦

Everything was working out perfectly for Bad News and Trouble. Since Terrell and Dee took the fall for the crime, they didn't even have to lay low.

After counting the money and drugs they got away with, and that was sitting really pretty, they realized it was $115,000 cash and 6 kilos of crack cocaine, street valued at a quarter of a million dollars.

The two lifelong friends had finally got away scot-free with the score of their lives, or so they thought. Trouble and Bad News were still laying low to an extent at Bad News's girlfriend's house in the Valley.

"Here's the plan; here's 50 thousand for you and 50 thousand for me. The other 15 will go toward weed. I got a connect in Cali for 5 pounds of Cali Kush for 15. We need that! We'll break it down one key at a time and sell it rock for rock at the trap house. Do nothing wholesale; we don't want to raise eyebrows or have any Jack Boys come looking for us. Let's stay low-key and take over the hood! Here," He handed Trouble a key of crack already broken down and individually wrapped. "You should be able to make 60 g's easy off of this. Bring all the cash back, and I'll give you another one," Bad News finished.

"Okay, what about you? What you gon' do?" Trouble asked.

"I'mma head to Cali to find us a cheap price on some work. What we have here will be gone in 3 months," Bad News said.

"Bet!" Trouble said.

"Don't fuck this up!" Bad News warned.

"I won't," Trouble assured.

Trouble headed back to the hood to set up shop at the trap house, which was his uncle's house. He let him sling out of the house in return for crack. However, Trouble didn't stay low-key for long. He bought a 56-inch flat screen and a PS3 for the trap house. He then had the audacity to get two cars, both fully equipped with 24-inch rims. As if that wasn't doing too much, he put some gold in his mouth and bought all new flashy clothes.

Trouble was really living life now. At the trap house, he and his cousin D'tre, the neighborhood drug dealer, would often play PS3 while smoking only the best weed all day, random girls stopping by all day and night, keeping both men thoroughly entertained. Clubbing was becoming essential, too. The money was so good now; Trouble had people working for him.

◆◆◆◆◆

Meanwhile, Dee and Terrell were in jail, still trying to figure out how the hell they got there, why they were still there, and wondering if they would ever get out!

Both Terrell and Dee pleaded not guilty to the murder and robbery charges; however, with both of their bonds set at close to a million dollars, needless to say, they remained in custody until the time for trial.

THREE

MONTHS WENT BY, AND Dee was having a hard time adjusting since he'd never been there. His mom came to visit often, supporting the fact that the truth would set them free. Terrell got frequent visits from Kelly; however, he hadn't seen his son in months due to his not wanting his son to see Daddy under his current conditions. Although, with every chance he got, he made sure Jr. heard his voice and vice versa.

Eventually, Kelly reluctantly informed Terrell of the visit she received from Trouble and Bad News and the threat that would have affected her life if she dared talk to the cops. Terrell assured her that everything would be alright once the truth came out in the trial.

With Kelly being his number one witness and the threat placed on her life, chances of her coming to court were slim to none. Plus, witnesses pointed both Dee and Terrell out in a lineup as the two men they saw running from the scene. Additionally, an anonymous tip led police to the discovery of the murder weapon.

On top of it all, with Terrell's star witness, his girlfriend, not testifying on their behalf, a jury of 12 found them guilty of all the charges. Terrell was sentenced to thirty years, but because it was Dee's first charge ever on top of his squeaky clean background, he was sentenced to twelve years in the state penitentiary.

The man robbed for the drugs, Oscar, was found to be part of the Mexican mafia, and when the word got out that Terrell and Dee were on their way to the State penitentiary, the Mexican mafia planned a hit on both of them.

The two were separated once they reached the State penitentiary. Terrell's cellmate was an older black guy named Porter and was serving the remaining one sentence from an initial six for vehicle assault.

Porter was a very religious guy who spent the majority of his day reading, working out, and meditating. Terrell was relieved. Dee, on the other hand, was placed in pod six, which was the worst pod to be in because it was infested with gang members, dope dealers, and troublemakers of all nationalities. He was bunked with a guy known as B.G., who was a gang banger from Compton, CA.

Dee walked into his cell for the first time and was immediately confronted by B.G.

"What's up, homie! What set you bang?" B.G. asked.

Dee, not wanting to seem intimidated, answered with his chest poked out, looking B.G. dead in his eyes. "I don't bang, homie."

"Cool. So, what brings you here?" B.G. asked.

"Nothing, I'm innocent," Dee replied.

"Yea, so is mostly everybody else in here. Let them tell it," B.G. said with a smirk.

"Naw, I really am *innocent*. I'm in here for a murder/robbery I did *not* commit. They say me and my boy robbed and killed a Mexican drug dealer," Dee said, exasperated.

"When was this?" B.G. asked.

"'Bout eight months ago," Dee replied.

"What was the Ese's name?" B.G. asked.

"Oscar," Dee answered.

"Oh shit! Oscar?! That was *You*?" B.G. exclaimed.

"How you know about it?" Dee asked, surprised.

"Man, the whole prison knows about it! They were hoping y'all would get sent here. Man, you say you don't bang; well, you better be careful. There's a hit out on you guys," B.G. told him.

"By who?" Dee asked in horror.

"Fool, the Mexican Mafia!"

Dee was terrified. Not only was he in jail for something he didn't do, but now he had to wonder if he'd survive while there. Trying to keep his voice calm, he asked B.G., "Damn! What should I do?"

"Man, you might have to join a gang for reinforcement," B.G. told him matter-of-factly.

"I'mma need to think about that," Dee returned.

"You do that," B.G. replied.

◆◆◆◆◆

Six months went by, and Terrell was depressed and never really came out of his cell. Kelly attempted to write and visit, but Terrell wouldn't write back nor accept her visits. He did, however, finally write only to tell her to move on with her life. He also told her that when Jr starts to ask questions concerning him, she should just tell him his daddy died. But Kelly continued to write and send pictures, keeping money on his books.

Terrell looked so different. He hadn't shaved or cut his hair since he'd been there. Word had gone out that the guys that killed Oscar were there, and plots were being made for Terrell and Dee's hit.

As reality kicked in just a little bit more, Dee became a part of a gang called the Piru Bloods for added protection. He remained alert as time slowly passed by.

Back on the streets, the police were able to lift prints off of the stolen and torched work van. After running all the names, only one name came back, not affiliated with the company, and that name was Marcus J Collins, aka Trouble. A warrant was immediately issued for his arrest for vehicle theft.

Trouble was not aware of the warrant, so he and Bad News were still up to no good. Bad News had gotten a major connect in Cali for some of the finest dope and weed, and business was booming. Bad News remained on the low, but Trouble just couldn't seem to stay out of "trouble!" Instead of staying posted and clockin' dollars, he was spending big cash and partying like a rock star. Dang near living in the strip clubs, making it "rain," constantly fighting over dice game money, slapping bitches, and smoking weed became part of Trouble's lifestyle, drawing a lot of attention to himself in every way possible and driving some of the cleanest cars.

One Monday evening, Trouble headed out to the valley to pick up the usual kilo of dope from Bad News, but instead of driving the low-key Honda Accord with the stash spot, he drove the low rider with the cherry paint and gold flakes with rims so shiny you could use them as a mirror. After 30 minutes in traffic, he finally arrived to meet Bad News.

Bad News opened the door, a .45 in hand, as Trouble knocked on his door.

"What's up, man?" Trouble greeted.

"Shit, sitting here watching sports center," Bad News replied.

"Damn, it smells good in here! What you smoking on?" Trouble asked.

"That's that O.G. Blue Berry here, roll one," Bad News told him.

"Naw, I'm trying to get back to the city before this traffic gets bad," Trouble said, declining the offer.

"Okay. It's on the table," Bad News told him.

Trouble grabbed the kilo and put it in his waistband. "Okay, I'm out!" he announced.

"Hold up, I'mma walk out with you. I need to go grab some blunt sticks," Bad News said.

Both men walked out of the two-level, bunched-together townhomes and out to the parking lot.

"Where's the car?" Bad News asked, looking around.

"Oh, I'm not in the Honda; I'm in that," Trouble said, pointing to his sparkly car parked illegally, custom-made just to his liking. It looked like something straight out of the Low Rider magazine.

"What the fuck?!" Bad News exclaimed. Trouble was so mesmerized by the beauty of his whip that he hadn't even noticed the aggression coming from Bad News. "Nigga you drove a fucking Low Rider on rims to the valley to pick up dope?! Are you out of your fuckin' mind!"

"Damn, chill out, homie. Everything's cool," Trouble replied.

"Chill out?! Hell naw, nigga! The streets are talking, and you're the main topic of conversation right now. Talking about how yow you flossing and how you doing these bitches. Check it! Don't ever pull some dumb shit like this again! We have a system; stick to it! I'll kill you before I let you fuck up my operation," Bad News warned exasperatedly.

"I thought it was *our* operation," Trouble said with annoyance.

"Aint shit ours! It's because of me we got all this shit, and it's my connect. You can be replaced nigga. Don't forget that!" Bad News retorted.

"It's like that my nig?" Trouble asked.

"It's just like that!" Bad News retorted.

"Man, I'm legit. I'm code four, and I have a license, registration, and legit insurance!" Trouble hopped in the car and sped off, only slowing down to go around the speed bumps in the parking lot. Bad News watched while standing in the parking lot, shaking his head. Long after Trouble was out of sight, he could still hear the faint music that was blaring so loud from Trouble's Low Rider as he sped off; even if you didn't see him, you definitely heard him.

After about twenty minutes on the highway, Trouble exits the 170 freeway on Holly headed south. As he entered the neighborhood, he saw some girls he knew walking down the street. Trying to floss in front of the females, he turned his tunes up and hit his switches, not aware that the police were behind him watching the show as well.

Just as his car bounced back to its normal position, the police hit their siren and lights. No big deal to Trouble; he was legit. The worst that could happen was he would get a ticket for disturbing the peace because his beats were knocking, or so he thought.

The officer approached the car with the standard request for a license, registration, and insurance.

"Not a problem, officer. here you go." Trouble handed the officer his paperwork.

"Do you know why I pulled you over, young man?" the officer asked.

"No, sir, I do not," Trouble answered.

"Your music was too loud. There is a noise ordinance in this neighborhood, and the volume of your music was not in compliance," the officer informed him.

"I understand, sir," Trouble replied.

"Okay. I will run everything, and if everything checks out, I will let you go with a warning. Gimme a sec," the officer told Trouble.

"No problem," Trouble replied.

The officer returned to his squad car while Trouble patiently waited. As the officer submitted Marcus Jones's information, a warrant popped up for vehicle theft. The officer called in another squad car for assistance. Shortly after, the other squad car pulled up directly in front of Trouble, blocking him.

Trouble suddenly got a little nervous because he swore he was code four. Trouble looked around as he thought about running, but the first officer was walking back to his car.

"Can you please step out of the car, Marcus?" the officer asked calmly.

"What's the problem, officer?" Trouble asked.

"Just step out of the car and put your hands on top of your head."

Trouble slipped the car door open and attempted to run but was caught immediately and wrestled to the ground by three officers. They cuffed him and put him in the back of the squad car, then proceeded to search his car and found a .45 gun and a kilo of crack cocaine. Needless to say, Trouble was hauled off to jail, and a tow company was called to remove his car from the location.

Back at the station, Trouble was questioned about the drugs, but he told them he needed to speak with his lawyer and that he had nothing else to say. Mr. Collins, aka Trouble, was then booked with charges of possession of a firearm and controlled substance.

Trouble knew this was not good and started to think about what he was going to tell Bad News. He called Bad News, who already got word that he was taken into custody.

"You have a collect call from "Trouble" at the Denver County Jail facility. To accept these charges, press—" Before the automation could continue, Bad News pressed 1.

"Hello?" Trouble said immediately.

"Look, I already know. I got a lawyer on it. Don't tell them shit. You might have to sit it down for a minute, but don't talk!" Bad News said.

"Okay," Trouble agreed.

Bad News went on to hire one of the best lawyers, but because of the crackdown on drugs, he wasn't able to get off easy. After months of going to trial and $15,000 in lawyer fees, the DA offered a deal because this was Trouble's first offense as an adult. He was offered eight years in the State penitentiary. Trouble agreed to the deal.

♦♦♦♦♦

Terrell and Dee had done a year and six months so far on their sentences, but the hit was still out on them. With Dee a part of the blood gang and Terrell still not really leaving his cell, it had been a task to get them.

Dee worked in the kitchen. On that fateful day, at about 3 am, they were in the middle of preparing breakfast when Dee went to the freezer to get the milk, unaware of the two Mexicans following him. Simultaneously, both men pulled out their prison-made shanks, attacked Dee, and left him there to die.

Another worker heard the commotion and ran to the scene. As he entered the freezer area, he saw Dee bleeding on the ground and yelled for help. It was too late. 19-year-old Deondre Sanders died from multiple stab wounds. What was nothing more than a hit appeared to be a racial thing between the Mexicans and the blacks, and word spread fast throughout the prison.

When Terrell heard about what happened to Dee, he was terrified, mad, and confused. He instantly blamed himself for what happened to Dee. He felt like he had such a bright future. Terrell went into severe depression and was now in a cell by himself because his cellmate was released not long ago. Not knowing what to expect from a new cellmate, he prayed it was somebody who would just leave him alone and be quiet.

A week after Dee was murdered, Terrell's cell door opened, and in walked his new cellmate, who was none other but Trouble.

FOUR

"DON'T I KNOW YOU from somewhere?" Trouble asked his new cellmate.

Terrell half glanced at him and said, "I don't know," but as he looked a little closer, he added, "You do look familiar, and I never forget a face."

"It will come sooner or later," Trouble told Terrell.

"Yea," Terrell replied.

"So, how long you got?" Trouble probed.

"Look, man, no disrespect, but I don't tell all my business, and I'm not trying to make any new friends. I keep to myself, just trying to do my time, and that's it." Terrell was straightforward.

"Have it your way." Trouble didn't recognize Terrell because of his new look. Terrell still hadn't shaved, so at this point, he was looking like an entirely different person.

♦♦♦♦♦

Months later, Trouble still didn't know what brought Terrell to jail. He made all types of attempts to get Terrell to open up, but nothing worked. Trouble couldn't help but notice something was really wrong with this man. He didn't open his mail, and he didn't put up pictures. He didn't have visits, shave, make phone calls, or anything.

One day, after coming home from working out, the two got into an argument because Terrell thought Trouble was being too loud while he was trying to sleep. Trouble had turned the radio on, and Terrell got up and turned it off. Trouble then turned it on again, and Terrell turned it off again.

"Look, nigga, I'm tired of you sleeping all the time, walking around this mutha fucka depressed and sad like it's the end of the world!" Trouble said.

Terrell hopped out of his bed and got in Trouble's face. "Fuck you nigga. You do your time your way, and I will do mine the way I want to."

"The problem with that is I can't. You're making my time hard. The last thing a nigga wanna see in jail is a sad, depressed mutha fucka who don't laugh, don't joke, and don't play cards. You just walk around acting like a bitch all day, and I'm sick of it! You did the crime, do the time nigga! There's people in here with life without parole that sit, laugh, and joke all day. If they knew how you act, they'd probably spank yo ass! At least you have light at the end of the tunnel!" Trouble said.

"That's just it. I'm here for a crime I did *not* commit. I'm innocent!" Terrell retorted.

Trouble laughed. "Yea, you and errbody else in here. Think about what I said. I'm 'bout to hit the shower." Trouble walked out of the cell.

Days after that argument, some of the things Trouble said started to wear on Terrell. That fateful Monday, Terrell was in the shower, and Trouble was brushing his teeth. Terrell noticed two Mexican mafia members whom he had never seen in his unit acting really suspiciously. He watched them in the mirror when he noticed them pulling their shanks out. They suddenly burst into Terrell's shower, and Terrell began shuffling with the two.

Immediately, Trouble ran over to help. Both men were stabbed by the mafia but managed to fight them off until the guards came and broke them up. Both Terrell and Trouble were taken to the infirmary and treated for their wounds.

Afterward, both men returned to their rooms after being questioned about the attack. Terrell knew it was a hit but claimed it was racially motivated.

"Awe, man, thanks!" Terrell told Trouble.

"No problem, you're my celly," Trouble replied.

"Naw, for real. I'd be dead right now if you hadn't come help get them fools off me," Terrell said. "And I have been thinking about what you said the other day, and I have been acting like an ass. I owe you tremendously."

"Fa Sho. You wanna know how you can repay me? Come out your shell and come play some ball wit a nigga in the yard tomorrow," Trouble challenged.

"But—but—" Terrell stammered.

"You said you owe me!" Trouble yelled.

"Okay," Terrell agreed.

The two made a pretty good team at basketball. They also made good spade partners. As time went on, the two got a little closer, but Terrell never really shared too much about his personal life. Trouble respected that, so he didn't ask anymore. Terrell even started reading Kelly's letters and even started writing back.

On the other hand, doing time was nothing to Trouble, who spent a lot of his childhood in and out of juvenile hall. The eight-year bid ain't shit to Trouble. He figured he'd only do about three and some change on that, and then he'd be back in the streets, and because he honored the "No snitch" rule, Bad News made sure his books were fat, and he knew half the jail population.

The months rolled by fast. The two men had now been cellmates for thirteen months and were starting to share stories about each other's lives.

May 15 was TJ's birthday, and Kelly sent Terrell pictures of her and TJ, along with pictures of the birthday party at Chucky Cheese. Over the month, Terrell shared with Trouble that he had a girl and a son, but there was nothing more detailed than that. But when he received the letter from Kelly, he couldn't wait to show his new buddy, Trouble.

After reading the letter, Terrell hopped off the bed and walked over to Trouble, who was reading a book.

"Aye man, this here is my lil man and his mom on his birthday," Terrell said handing Trouble the pictures.

Trouble's mouth dropped as he recognized Kelly and Terrell's son. Trouble thought to himself, *"No, this can't be!"*

"You okay? You look like you just saw a ghost." Terrell couldn't hide his concern.

"Naw, I'm cool. Lil man looks just like you, my nig. Ain't no denying that one!" Trouble said.

"Yea, these two are my world." Terrell tried to hold back the tear that had formed in his eyes as he stared at the picture. "She was my high school sweetheart. We were planning on getting married right before all this crazy shit popped off. Now, my seed gotta grow without a father like I did," Terrell paused. "Man, my bad for getting all sentimental, but it's been tough on me being in here knowing I shouldn't, and ain't shit I can do about it. You've been the closest thing to a friend since I've been here."

"Awe man, you 'bout to make me cry. Ha ha. I'm 'bout ta hop in the shower," Trouble said.

"Thanks for listening," Terrell said.

"Fa sho!" Trouble gathered his clothes and walked to the shower. While he was in the shower, he punched the wall so hard. "Damn!

What the fuck is the chances of this shit?! And what the fuck am I going to do?" He asked himself out loud. He decided not to tell Terrell. But as time passed and they got closer, his conscience started eating at him.

Terrell started to put up pictures; he also put one up of Dee. When Trouble saw Dee's picture, he inquired about it.

"Aye, man, is that your brother?" Trouble asked.

Terrell put his head down and shook his head.

"Naw, man, that's my partner Dee. RIP. We was close. He was like a little brother to me, though," Terrell replied.

"What happened to him?" Trouble asked again.

"Remember I told you I didn't commit the crime I'm in here for?" Terrell started.

"Yea," Trouble replied.

"I've never told you this, but I'm here for killing some well-known Mexican drug dealer, and my boy Dee was my co-defendant, the other person that 'supposedly' was with me. Long story short, 'bout a year after we'd been here..." Terrell could feel his eyes watering up. "Some Mexicans killed him."

"Who? The Mexican mob?" Now, Trouble's wheels were spinning. "Oh, so that explains why them Eses was trying to take you out in the shower!"

"Yea, and it's messed up because he really had a bright future ahead of him. He was on his way to college, LSU, to play ball. My boy was a straight-A student, my nig. Even though he was younger than me, I looked up to him. Damn! All this because of bad timing!" Terrell said.

"Man! There has got to be a way for you to get out of this situation!" Trouble said. He was so caught up in Terrell's reflection that, for a slight moment, he forgot that that should have been him instead of Dee.

"Yea, if the real killers come forth." Terrell shook his head and laughed at the far-fetched thought of that ever happening. "And what are the chances of that ever happening? Anyway, I think I'm finally ready to see my son. I'm thinking 'bout telling his mom to plan a visit on Easter with my mom. I can't wait to see them!" Terrell said with a smile. "Thanks to you, man, I ain't all sad and depressed no more. I can finally make the best out of this situation. I may not have freedom, but I still have life. I can't wait for you to meet them."

Trouble smiled a nervous smile and attempted to steady his voice as he replied, "Yea, me either."

Business was booming on the streets! Bad News was wondering why he hadn't heard from Trouble. Trouble was up for parole in a year, and Bad News had planned on surprising his ole pal with a visit on Easter. He wanted to let him know the big plans he had for him when he got out and to thank him personally for not snitching.

FIVE

THE DAY BEFORE EASTER, Terrell was super excited about his first visit with his son and his baby mamma. He expressed the hate he had towards the real killers that had him away from his son and first love and how his boy Dee got caught up in the bullshit.

It was right around noon, and everybody was waiting for their names to be called. After what seemed to be hours but was really mere minutes, Terrell's name was called over the loud P.A. system. Just as Trouble was wishing Terrell a happy visit, his name was called, too.

"Who the hell could be coming to see me?" Trouble asked, bewildered.

"Man, it don't matter! You can get out this cell, and you can meet my people!" Trouble said, unable to hide his excitement.

Trouble's whole world came to a halt. His heart pumped so hard he could swear it could be heard outside his chest. He quickly tried to come up with a response and excuse. Anything! If it were Bad News in the waiting area, they would for sure be recognizable to Terrell's baby momma.

Trouble thought of declining the visit but remembered it was a two-hour drive to the facility. Going into brain overload, he said, "Aye, Terrell, I got something I need to tell you."

"Wassup man, can't it wait?" Terrell asked impatiently.

"Naw, dude, it can't," Trouble replied urgently.

Terrell kept shuffling, trying to do last-minute fixtures, wanting to look as presentable as he possibly could, being that this was the first time he'd be seeing his family in years.

"What's so important that it can't wait till after our visits?" Terrell asked impatiently.

Trouble deciding to just tell Terrell the truth, he opened his mouth, then closed it again. "I can't," he said. Just as he was attempting to get it out finally, the guard came to the cell to see what was taking the men so long to come out. Terrell rushed out of the cell, yelling behind him, "Say, just tell me later, k?"

Trouble stood there frozen in the same spot in a daze when his thoughts were interrupted by the guard, who was now getting impatient.

"What chu gon' do boy? I ain't got all day. You want to decline the visit or what?" the guard asked irritably.

"Fuck! Here I come," Trouble said.

Exhausted from the long 2-hour trip, Bad News sat as still as he possibly could, paranoid by the presence of all the guards swarming about the facility. Approximately three tables down were Terrell's mom, baby momma, and son talking amongst themselves while looking forward to their long-awaited visit.

Just then, Terrell walked in, looking extra happy and excited. He gave all three big hugs and kisses but squeezed Jr. a little tighter and told him how much he loved and had missed him.

Trouble finally walked in with his head down and hands covering his face, not wanting to be recognized by Terrell's baby momma or son. However, with the emotion at Terrell's table, nobody even looked Trouble's way.

Trouble scanned the room to see who came to visit when he noticed Bad News all geared up, waving his arm so Trouble could see him. Trouble approached his table and plopped down.

"What you doing here?" Trouble asked, still nervous.

"What?! I drove two hours to come see my peeps, and all you have to say is, 'What you doing here?' Damn!" Bad News said, then continued. "How are you nigga? I know you straight, considering I keep ya books heavy."

"My bad. Being locked up can take a toll on a nigga," Trouble replied.

"I can feel that," Bad News said.

The two men continued to chop it up. Three tables away, Terrell's visit was also going awesome.

"I'm so glad to see your spirits up. I'm even more glad you allowed us a visit," Kelly told Terrell, love and happiness shining in her eyes.

"Yea, baby. It's always easier when you have family by your side to get you through tough times," Terrell's mom added.

"I can't lie; I owe major credit to that guy over there," Terrell said, pointing to Trouble, who had his back slightly turned to them.

"Who? *We* owe him credit!" Kelly said, chuckling lightly as she looked in the direction Terrell was pointing in. Just then, Trouble looked over his shoulder. Kelly's mouth dropped as she stared as if she just saw a ghost.

"Oh my God! Are you freakin' kidding me!" Kelly exclaimed.

"What's wrong?" Terrell asked.

"That's them! Those are the bastards who threatened me and TJ and told me not to talk to the cops," Kelly remarked, anger evident in her voice.

Bad News looked up and noticed the people staring their way. "Who the fuck is that, Trouble?"

Terrell stared in shock at both men. At that very moment, he had a flashback to the day Dee, and he ran by those two guys coming out of a house two doors down from Kelly's.

"It's them!" Terrell screamed and hit the table in rage. Terrell's mom and Kelly tried to calm him down.

The guard walked up and warned, "One more loud outburst, and you're going back to your cell!"

"Damn, what's his problem? Wait a minute, is that Kelly? What is she doing up here? That must be her baby daddy," Bad News started to laugh. "That's crazy! Trouble, do he know who you are? Because if not, he does now."

"It's worse than that; he's my cellmate," Trouble said sadly.

"For real? He's going to fuck you up! Hahaha…" Bad News laughed.

"That's not funny. He's in here for a crime that he didn't commit," Trouble said firmly.

"Yea, stupid, because we did it! But anyway, forget him, you just do your time and keep your mouth shut! You only have one more year to go, and you're out of here. Forget that buster; he could sit in here and rot in jail!" Bad News remarked.

"Yea, but it's just not right," Trouble said.

"What? Don't go soft on me now. Keep quiet, and things will be cool; open your mouth, and you'll be seeing your mom soon," Bad News said.

"Wrap it!" the guard yelled. "Back to your cells!"

Bad News gave Trouble a few daps and a handshake. Terrell gave little TJ a big hug, kissed Kelly goodbye, and gave his momma a long squeeze.

"Look, Terrell, don't do nothing stupid," Terrell's mom told him sternly.

"Okay, Mom," he replied.

After the visit time ended, the men returned to their cells. As soon as Terrell and Trouble walked into their cell, Terrell rushed Trouble some punches with a flurry of blows before Trouble could say a word.

"Calm down, calm down," Trouble yelled.

"I'm going to kill you! You ruined my life!" Terrell yelled.

After a long scuffle, both men got tired.

"How can you?" how long did you know I was in here for a crime *you* committed?" Terrell asked, feeling betrayed.

"It wasn't supposed to go down like that. I tried to tell you, but you didn't listen," Trouble said.

"You got to tell them I didn't commit that crime. You have to confess," Terrell said.

"It's not that simple. Even if I think about confessing, my partner, Bad News, will kill me. I'm sorry, I can't," Trouble told him.

"It's because of you Dee's dead!" Terrell exclaimed.

The men started to scuffle again. This time, it took the guard to break the two apart. Both men were punished and permanently separated for the fight.

After being separated and questioned about the fight, Trouble told the prison administrator that it was just a misunderstanding over some property.

After each man had done his time in a hole, Terrell gave Kelly a collect call. He urged her to get in touch with Detective Ford, the detective who worked his case.

"Why?" Kelly asked.

"We need to tell him that we have new information about my case," Terrell told her. Still, she refused to talk to Detective Ford because if she did, she thought somebody would try to kill her and her son.

Before getting off the phone, he made her promise that she'd get in touch with the detective. She made the promise, and they hung up the phone.

◆◆◆◆◆

Out on the street, Bad News made it a point to bump into Kelly everywhere she went. On her way to work, he would pass by, and when she got off work, he would pass by. One day, Kelly went to the store to buy some groceries. When she came out of the grocery store, Bad News was sitting on her car bonnet.

"What the hell are you doing? Leave me alone!" Kelly said, exasperated.

"What are you talking about? Can't an old friend help you put some groceries in the car? Where's your little son at? Oh, that's right, you don't go pick him up until six," Bad News said.

"Why do you keep harassing me? What is it that you want from me?" Kelly asked.

"Don't talk to no police!" he warned and walked away.

Kelly, scared of what had just happened, rushed to the daycare to pick up little Terrell. Then, she rushed over to Terrell's mother's house to tell her what had just happened.

"I don't know what to do. I'm scared for me and my baby's life," Kelly told Terrell's mom.

"Terrell called; he wants to know if you got in touch with Detective Ford at District Two homicide division. I think that you should pay him a visit tomorrow and see what he can do to help us," Terrell's mom said.

"No, but I can't. If I go to the cops, he'll kill me!" Kelly exclaimed, terrified.

"But we have to, Kelly. Somebody got to stand up to these thugs. Dee's dead, and I'm not going to lose my son! We're just going to have to stick together. Trust me, baby; this will all come to pass," Terrell's mom assured.

A week passed, and Kelly had been calling and leaving messages on Detective Ford's phone. Detective Ford would listen to the messages but wonder what she could possibly be calling about; this case was four years old now. He remembered this was his first case of homicide, but it had been solved. *"That's the case that put me on a map!"* he thought. He was never totally convinced that the suspects he convicted of the crime had done it. *"Maybe I should hear her out,"* he thought, then he shook his head. "Nah!" he concluded to himself.

After receiving no response from Detective Ford, Kelly decided to pay him a visit. By 9 am on a Tuesday, Kelly walked into the police station holding TJ's hand, demanding to talk to Detective Ford.

SIX

"I WANT TO SEE Detective Ford. I have to see him today!" Kelly demanded.

"He's not here yet. He'll be here any minute now. You can have a seat," the receptionist told her.

"I sure will," Kelly responded in a ghetto tone.

After fifteen minutes, Detective Ford walked in with coffee and donuts in his hand. He greeted his staff and walked by Kelly. As Kelly sat there, she heard somebody speaking, "Good morning, Detective Ford."

Kelly immediately sprung up, got in his path, and asked him, "Are you Detective Ford?" Kelly asked.

"Yes! How can I help you?" Detective Ford asked.

"Why don't you check your messages or return phone calls? I'm Kelly, Terrell's baby mama. What? You don't remember Terrell? You should! You put him in jail for a crime that he didn't commit!" Kelly raised her voice.

"Okay, come down and step into my office," Detective Ford said.

Kelly walked into his office and he closed the door. "Now, what's all this about?" Detective Ford asked.

"It's about who really killed Oscar!" Kelly said.

"I suppose you know," Detective Ford said.

"Yes, I do! It was Trouble and Bad News," she said.

"Why are you telling me this now? You had your chance to be a witness in court," Detective Ford pointed out.

"I know, but I was so young and scared. They came by my house and threatened my life," Kelly defended.

"So why are you telling me this now?" he asked.

"Because Trouble and Terrell are in jail, and I'm scared that he might try to do something stupid. Please help us; little TJ needs his dad," Kelly told him.

"It sounds good, but you just can't reopen a case that has been closed for years just because two people are in jail together. I need more than that. Something like a confession, some hard evidence. Did you see Trouble or Bad News that day of the crime?" Detective Ford asked.

"No, but Terrell did," Kelly replied.

"What about the getaway vehicle?" he asked again.

"No, but maybe the cable man seen something. I seen a cable truck out front that day," she answered.

"Is that all?" he asked.

"Yes, that's all I can think of," Kelly replied.

"I'm afraid that without any hard evidence, I have no reason to look into this 'Trouble' guy. But I'll look into this cable van and see if it was somebody working that day that seen anything, but other than that, you have nothing. I'm sorry," Detective Ford said with an air of finality.

"Yea, I bet." Kelly got up and grabbed TJ by the hand. "Come on, TJ."

Kelly walked out of the police station. She strapped TJ in a car seat and then hopped in the car. Unknown to her, Bad News was parked in an SUV watching her. She pulled off, and Bad News pulled off in pursuit, following after her.

After ten minutes of pursuit, he decided to make his move on the road. He drove alongside Kelly. He then pulled out a gun and aimed it. When she looked over and noticed Bad News pointing a gun at her, she panicked and turned the wheel real hard, causing the car to somersault two times.

Bad News popped out of the car and walked up to Kelly's car to finish her off, but as he walked up to the car to shoot her, a witness rolled up and asked him if he was alright. He put his gun back in his waist, went back to his car, and left the scene.

The witness called 911, and both Kelly and TJ were rushed to the hospital. As paramedics and police officers arrived at the scene, one of the patrol officers recognized Kelly from the police station earlier that day and immediately contacted Detective Ford.

Detective Ford picked up the phone.

"This is Officer Armstrong," the officer said.

"Yes, how can I help you?" Detective Ford asked.

"Yea. Didn't you meet with Kelly Jackson today?" the officer asked.

"Yes, as a matter of fact, I did," Detective Ford replied.

"What? She just got into a terrible car accident. It seems like somebody tried to take her out," the officer said.

"What?!" Detective Ford yelled. "Is she okay? What about the baby?"

"There was nobody dead at the scene, but it didn't look too good. They were rushed to Martin Luther King Hospital on the south side," the officer replied.

"Okay, thanks," Detective Ford said.

Detective Ford grabbed his coat off the back of his chair and headed to the hospital. He ran into the emergency room and grabbed the first nurse he saw. "Can you help me? I'm looking for a young lady and a child who were in an accident. can you tell me where they are?" Detective Ford asked.

"Sure. The little boy is in Room 201, but the mom was rushed to trauma," the nurse said.

"Are they okay?" Detective Ford said.

"The child is okay, but it doesn't look too good for the mother. She doesn't look like she'll make it." The nurse replied.

"Can I see her?" he asked.

"I'm afraid not," the nurse replied.

"Can I see the kid?" he asked again.

"No, not without consent from the next of kin. But you are welcome to wait," the nurse told him.

Detective Ford stood there in a daze for a minute, then he walked outside and lit a cigarette. After pacing for a few minutes and rubbing his head, he decided to head back to the station to gather information from the officers who arrived on the scene.

The hospital notified the family of the incident, and in a short while, the family arrived at the hospital, including Terrell's mother. The doctor came out and notified the family that TJ was suffering from a broken arm and a small concussion.

Then the doctor delivered the bad news.

"I'm sorry, but Kelly is in a coma, and the chances of her making it are slim," the doctor said.

The family was full of sorrow, especially Kelly's sister, Dina, who broke down crying.

♦♦♦♦♦

Detective Ford's shift was over at the station, and he decided to head to the hospital to find out Kelly's condition. As he walked into the waiting room of the hospital, he found himself surrounded by a grieving family. Detective Ford gave the family his condolences and assured them that he would do everything in his power to find out who did this.

He left the hospital in sorrow and headed to the local bar, where all the cops hang out. Detective Ford walked into the bar and took a seat.

"Is it a rough day at the station today, Detective?" the bartender asked.

Detective Ford rubbed his head and answered, "You don't know the half of it. Let me get the usual, but this time, make it a double!" Detective Ford replied.

"Okay, one double shot of a Seagrum 7 is coming up," the bartender replied.

Detective Ford picked up his glass, threw the drink down his throat in one gulp, slammed the glass on the table, and asked for another double shot. Before his drink arrived, Detective Ford suddenly had an idea. He then picked up his phone and called an old partner who was down in the gang unit.

"Hello?" Davies, Detective Ford's friend, said.

"What's up, old buddy? How are they treating you down there in the streets?" Detective Ford asked, sounding drunk.

"Ford, how you doing, big shot? I see you still solving murder cases," Davies said.

"Yea, but I need a favor," Detective Ford replied.

"Okay. What you need, old pal?" Davies asked.

"I need you to pull up everything you have on file on two gang members. One's name is Trouble, and the other's is Bad News," Detective Ford told him.

"Okay, I'll see what I can do," Davies said.

"Man, I really need you on this one. Can you meet me at the Old Spot?" Detective Ford asked.

"The old hang-out?" Davies asked.

"Yea," Detective Ford replied.

"Sure," Davies agreed.

Forty-five minutes into the night, the bar started to fill up with cops. Detective Ford was playing pool. Davies walked into the bar, and the bartender pointed in Detective Ford's direction. As soon as he saw Detective Ford, Davies walked up to him and threw a 100-dollar bill on the table.

"I got $100 that he'll whip your ass!" Davies said jokingly, talking about Detective Ford's opponent.

Detective Ford responded with a chuckle. He put some chalk at the end of the stick, bent over, concentrated, and then banked the eight ball into the corner pocket. "I still got it," he said.

They greeted each other with a hug and a handshake.

"Let's have a seat over here! What you got for me?" Detective Ford asked. Davies handed Detective Ford a folder that contained both individuals' backgrounds.

"Well, it seems like you got your hands on some real knuckleheads this time. Bad News recently got out of jail after doing eight years for armed robbery. His criminal history dates back to when he was a juvenile. Trouble has a history of breaking into homes and stealing cars; he's actually in jail now, serving time for car theft and being in possession of drugs." Davies pointed to the folder and said, "It's all there!"

Detective Ford read through the folder and saw that Trouble had stolen a van. "Wait a minute," he said to himself, then he remembered Kelly telling him that it was a van outside her house the morning of the murder. He also read the amount of cocaine that was seized. "Son of a b****! She was telling the truth!" Detective Ford said out loud. He shook Davies's hand. "Thanks, man. I owe you big time for this one. Sorry to rush off, but I have to go!" Detective Ford said and returned to the station to dig up the hard facts about the information he just obtained.

Detective Ford worked overnight till the morning, anticipating the arrival of his supervisor. As soon as his boss, Cpt Lee, arrived, he rushed into the office to tell him the news. He knocked on the door and waited for Cpt Lee to say his usual "Come in!"

Detective Ford walked in and put a folder on the Captain's desk. "We need to talk about the Oscar Velasquez case," Detective Ford said.

"Velasquez? That doesn't ring a bell," Captain Lee said.

"I know that's because the case is over five years old," Detective Ford said.

"Is it a cold case?" Captain Lee asked.

"No, the case is closed; we solved it. But I'm pretty sure we convicted two innocent people," Detective Ford replied.

"Now, how the hell did you manage to do that?" Captain Lee asked.

"It was my first case; I was working with Detective Smith, a veteran detective who made it seem like this was an open and shut case. If you ask me, the son of a bitch was prejudiced!" Detective Ford remarked.

"Watch your mouth! Detective Smith was one of the best damn detectives this department has ever seen, and I will not let you disgrace his name by opening a case that was deemed solved. Do you know how much heat you'll bring to the department? You're talking media and millions in lawsuits! Do yourself a favor, Detective Ford; let it go!" Captain Lee advised.

"I can't do that, sir; we ruined two kids' lives because we didn't do our job! One of these boys died, and the other one is going to lose his life if we just sit back and do nothing. I took an oath to protect and serve the innocent, so if I have to lose everything I worked for to save a life, then so be it!" Detective Ford said.

"You're going to regret this!" Captain Lee said. He picked up the phone. "Get me the District Attorney's office," he said into the phone.

"Thank you, Captain!" Detective Ford said, and then he returned to his office. The first thing on his agenda was to pay Trouble a visit so he could interrogate him on his whereabouts the morning of the murder.

Early in the morning the next day, Detective Ford headed to the prison to talk to Terrell about reopening his case and to ask him about his whereabouts the morning of the murder.

Detective Ford arrived at the prison for a confidential visit with Terrell, but when he saw Terrell, he didn't get the reaction he expected.

"Hello, Terrell. I'm Detective Ford. I was the assistant detective on your case a few years back," Detective Ford said.

"Okay, so what's this about?" Terrell asked nonchalantly.

"Have a seat, and we'll get to that. First off, I want to start by giving you my condolences. It was unfortunate what happened to your fiance and son. Were you aware that she came to visit me the morning of the accident?"

"No! Well, she did," Detective Ford said. "Now, I'm thinking that this wasn't an accident but an attempt to take her life!"

Terrell jumped out of his seat in anger. "What! They tried to kill my family?"

"Wait a minute, calm down. We don't know that yet; we're just saying that it's a strong possibility. Fortunately for you, she provided us with some information that might help you get out of jail. But first, I'm going to need you to answer a couple of questions," Detective Ford told him.

"What answers to some questions?! You got nerve enough to come in here and ask for my help? Hell no!" Terrell said.

"Look, man, I'm trying to get you out of here," Detective Ford assured.

"OK, so now you want to do your job? What, you going to give Dee his life back? And what about my life, huh? You going to fix that?" Terrell retorted.

"Honestly, the only person I care about is your son, Tarell Jr. He already lost his mom. He doesn't deserve to lose you too. Don't do it for me; do it for him," Detective Ford told him.

Tarell dropped his head. "Yea, l know. Poor little dude, he doesn't even know what's going on." Terrell agreed to answer the questions, and he described in detail everything that happened on the day of Oscar's murder. He even told him how Trouble and he made eye contact as he was running for the bus stop.

"Thanks," Detective Ford said. "Hold on. I'll get you out of here if it's the last thing I do."

Terrell was escorted back to his cell. Then, the C/O summoned Trouble. Trouble walked in and took the seat across Detective Ford.

Before Detective Ford could utter a word, Trouble spoke. "So, what's this about?"

"I'm the only one asking questions here! But since you asked, it's about murder," Detective Ford replied testily.

"Murder? How the fuck am I going to know something about a murder, and I have been sitting in jail for four years? Man, get the hell out my face!" Trouble retorted.

"Well, see, this murder happened five years ago, and it got your name written all over it. I am talking about Oscar Velasquez. Street name: Big O." Detective Ford said. "You see before Kelly died, she gave us some information that helped us link you directly to the murder."

"Bullshit!" Trouble yelled.

"Are your fingerprints on the getaway car some bullshit? What about the drugs that were found on you this time? I linked that back to Oscar's cartel. It's over for you, Marcus," Detective Ford told him.

"So, if you got me red-handed, why are we here? I know you didn't bring me in here to give me new charges. They would've sent me a court date!" Trouble retorted.

"Smart guy! I'll cut straight through the chase. I want Bad News. I don't care about no drug dealer who dies in the street; they choose that life. It's about what he did to Kelly and little Terrell. When you target innocent women and children, that is when I get involved. You see, I did my homework on you, Marcus Jones..." Detective Ford opened a folder sitting on the desk. "And you're not a thug. You grew up in a good home, and you made good grades. I see here you had a scholarship to play basketball, but instead, you chose to hang with the wrong crowd. Yea, you had a couple of run-ins with the law, but nothing serious—burglary and motor vehicle theft in '05. See, you're what we call a petty thief; you're not a killer."

Detective Ford put away Trouble's file. He then opened Bad News's file. "Now, Damien Ross, a.k.a Bad News? He is another story. Possession of a firearm, assault with a deadly weapon, he beat a murder charge in '06 because the witness wouldn't cooperate. You see, now, that's a killer. What I don't understand is how a smart kid like you gets wrapped up with an individual like this."

"Man, that's like my brother. My mother took him in when his mother died," Trouble told Detective Ford.

"You must have a really good mother; how do you think she's going to feel when you go down for murder? That's going to break her heart! Think about it—first Degree Murder with drugs involved! After I get done with you, you'll be lucky if you get 20 years! But I have a feeling you didn't do it, so tell me what happened. Did things go bad, and Bad News lost it and killed Oscar?" Detective Ford asked again.

"Man, I don't know what you're talking about," Trouble replied.

"So that's how you wanna play it? You're just gonna be Bad News's little bitch?" Detective Ford asked.

"Man, I'm not anybody's bitch!" Trouble exclaimed.

"I can't tell. He's at home and probably eating a T-bone steak right now. What are *you* doing? And you're going to be here for 20 years if you are lucky, all for somebody who don't give a damn about you! Can't you see what he is doing? You were going somewhere in life, and you let him take all that away! Marcus, please do the right thing for once in your life and get this killer off the streets before he ruins more lives," Detective Ford implored.

Trouble shook his head. "Man, I don't know."

"This is what I'm going to do for you. I'm going to give you 72 hours to make your mind up. You either give me Bad News, or we charge you with the murder of Oscar Velasquez." Detective Ford looked at the guard and said, "Get this punk out of my face."

The guard escorted Trouble back to his cell while Detective Ford headed back to the station in hopes that his words got through to Trouble. "There is nothing we can do but wait," he told his partner.

♦♦♦♦♦

Things changed for the worse for Kelly. She was now on life support. The doctor called the family to update them on her status. He informed them that due to the head trauma she sustained from the accident, Kelly was now brain-dead.

Kelly's mother decided to take her off of life support, but before she did, she, Kelly's sister, Dana, and her grandson, Terrell Junior, went to say their final goodbye. The last person to speak to her was Terrell Jr.

"I love you, Mom," he said and then kissed her on the cheek.

Kelly's mom then gave the permission to pull Kelly off of life support.

After a few seconds, Kelly passed away.

The following day, Terrell phoned his mom and learned the shocking news; he was devastated.

"No! No!" he cried. "Where is little TJ?" he asked.

"He's okay, baby. He's with Kelly's mom right now, but when I go and get him next week, we will be there to visit with you," his mother responded.

"Why? Why is this happening to me?" Terrell cried.

"I know it hurts, son, but you have to be strong. God won't put you through anything you can't handle. Just pray," his mom tells him.

"I'm tired of praying, mama. I can't take this shit no more!" Terrell told his mom.

"Stop talking like that!" Terrell's mom rebukes.

"This time, these motherfuckers are going to pay!" He slammed the phone down and walked away. When he got back to his cell. "Get the fuck out!" he told his younger cellmate.

"What did I do wrong?" his cellmate asked.

"Just get the fuck out," Terrell said.

His cellmate left the cell. In a rage, Terrell punched the wall until he couldn't anymore; he then turned around with his back against the wall and slid down the wall. After about an hour, he calmed down, thought about how he could get revenge on Trouble, and came up with a plan.

"I know what I'll do," Terrell said to himself. "I'll go to the Mexican Mafia and tell them that Trouble really killed Oscar. I'll tell them what really happened that day. That way, he'll get killed just like Dee."

He knew it was risky, but he figured he had nothing to lose. He planned to do it first thing the next day at the yard call. As the night passed by, Terrell was restless. He couldn't sleep. He kept thinking about Kelly dying and his revenge on Trouble.

♦♦♦♦♦

The next morning came, and the staff prepared and served breakfast. After eating breakfast and cleaning up, the first-yard call of the day was called. Terrell immediately put his plan into effect.

Angel was the leader of the Mexican mafia. Every Mexican in jail answered to him; no assassinations or hits happened unless it had his approval, plus he was the one who was responsible for taking out the hit on Terrell.

Angel and his goons usually gathered around the bleachers near the basketball court. Angel, being the head honcho, sat at the top, surrounded and protected by his goons and young soldiers in case of an assassination attempt.

Terrell headed over to Angel, but before he got too close, he was stopped by a couple of Angel's soldiers.

"Hey! Hey!" one of the soldiers blurted out. "Are you fucking crazy or stupid, or do you just want to die?"

"Hey man, I really need to speak to Angel," Terrell replied.

"One second. Wait right here," one of the soldiers said, and he walked over to Angel, pointed to Terrell, and said a couple of words.

Angel looked over at Terrell and gave his soldier the approval to let Terrell approach. Before Terrell got to Angel, the soldiers pat him down to make sure he did not have a weapon. Then, they allowed him to pass.

Terrell walked over and sat next to Angel, who was looking away from Terrell.

"You got nerves, homie! This better be good!" Angel said.

"I didn't kill Oscar, Angel!" Terrell said.

"So what the fuck are you telling me for? Tell it to Judge Judy!" Angel replied.

"Listen to me. I know who did it, and they're in this jail. I just happened to be in the wrong place at the wrong time. I want revenge. I want him dead and you off of my back," Terrell informs Angel.

"Okay, what do you need from us?" Angel asked.

"I need your help. I need a shank and a way to get close to him," Terrell said.

"Okay," Angel said. "But one thing, if you don't kill him, we will kill you!"

"Okay, Angel. You will be hearing from me soon," Terrell said, and he got up and walked off.

◆◆◆◆◆

On the other side of the prison, Trouble got an unexpected visit from Bad News. Trouble walked up to the glass, picked up the phone, and sat down.

"What's up? How is my boy doing?"

"Nothing much, man. Ready to come home, that's all."

After catching up on other things, Trouble told Bad News about his visit from Detective Ford.

"Don't worry, I took care of that!" Bad News told him.

"What?!" Trouble exclaimed.

"Don't worry. I took care of that bitch Kelly!" Bad News repeated.

"What? Don't tell me you killed Kelly!" Trouble exclaimed.

"That's exactly what I'm telling you," Bad News replied.

Trouble banged the phone against his head. "No! No!" he repeated. "Bad News, I can't fucking believe you. When are you going to stop?! Can't you see you're ruining everyone's lives?"

"Sit down and shut up!" Bad News commanded.

"Nah, man, I'm done with you!" Trouble hung up the phone.

"You're not done with me! You need me! You better not snitch, you fucking punk!" Bad News yelled, slammed the phone on the hook, and headed out of the jail.

Trouble got to his cell and sat on his bunk with his mother's picture in his hand. Then, he pulled out a picture of little Terrell that he had stolen from Terrell when he moved out of his cell. He grabbed Detective Ford's business card and went to the phone. He dialed the number, but the call went unanswered, and the answering machine came on. Trouble left a message.

"This is Trouble. I'm ready to talk," he said, and then he hung up the phone.

Detective Ford received the message from Trouble the following day. He contacted the district attorney's office and told them the good news about the confession. A meeting was set up between the D.A.'s office and Trouble's lawyer to make a deal to give immunity for his confession. This meant he would receive no time in jail as long as he cooperated with authorities to convict Bad News.

Trouble and his lawyer agreed to the terms.

After the delegations, Trouble sat down with Detective Ford in the interrogation room. Detective Ford laid down a tape recorder on the table and pressed record.

"Case no 15823: State vs. Marcus Jones confession. State your name for the record," Detective Ford told Trouble.

"Marcus Jones," Trouble replied.

Mr. Scruggs, can you please tell us what happened on the morning of August 16, 2011?" Detective Ford interrogated.

Trouble started to tell the whole story in detail. After a 12-minute-long confession, Trouble finally finished. Detective Ford pressed stop on the tape recorder.

"You did the right thing," said Detective Ford. "On behalf of the Dallas police department and me, we thank you."

"Don't get it twisted; I didn't do this for you. Don't give a fuck about the police. I did this for me. And don't you forget that!" Trouble retorted.

The guard cuffed Trouble and took him back to his prison cell, where he would serve the rest of his sentence, which would be 28 days.

SEVEN

AN ARREST WARRANT WAS issued for Bad News, But when they went to his residence, he was long gone. So now Detective Ford had to get Terrell out of jail as soon as possible before the Mexican mafia would attempt to execute him or he did something stupid. It was now a race against the clock, and right now, he couldn't do anything without the judge's approval. This process could take up to two weeks. Time was ticking.

On Saturday morning, in the prison, mail called an inmate's mail and threw a package in his cell. Terrell got up to check his package. He noticed it felt heavy for a package that size. *"Very unusual,"* he thought.

He sat on his bunk and opened the package. Inside, he found a shank and a note from Angel. The note read:

Here's your opportunity. He will be working in the laundry room tomorrow at 2:00 pm. I will arrange for the door to be unlocked.

Oh, and remember, it's either him or you! Also, please return this note to the person who delivered this message.

Terrell handed over the letter without the shank and lay it on his bunk.

Tossing and turning in his bed, Terrell wondered how the hell he got himself in this mess. Feeling uneasy, he got up and paced the floor back and forth, back and forth. This got the attention of his new cellmate.

Terrell's cellmate was an older AA gentleman from Compton.

He was serving a 25 to life for shooting at the police. Now, this guy right here was cool, laid back, and didn't really talk much. All he did was go to work and exercise every day. His name was Spank. Everybody in the jailhouse considered him wise, given that he had already been there for 18 years.

Spank sat up in his bed. "What's up, youngster? What's on your mind?" he asked Terrell.

"Not today, O.G.," Terrell responded.

"I don't see why not; we ain't got nothing but time, and the way you're pacin' the floor seems like you're running out of time," Spank replied. He hopped off his bed and continued speaking. "Speaking of time, a matter of fact, it takes but a second to make a mistake. Think about it: You trade your whole life for how you feel in the moment and then spend your whole life in jail, regretting your actions and wishing you could get that moment back. Maybe you just need to take a moment and think about the rest of your life."

"Yea, I hear you, O.G.," Terrell responded.

Terrell lay on his bed, thinking. Minutes passed before he dozed off to sleep. While asleep, he had a dream in which he got a visit from Kelly. In the dream, she told him to be there for Terrell Junior.

"But he's going to need you," Terrell whined.

"I'm okay; just be there for your son," Kelly said calmly.

Terrell woke up from the dream and started having memories of them hanging out and spending time. And just like that, time was up.

It was lunchtime, time to make the hit. *"Oh man,"* he thought to himself. *"What am I going to do? If I don't make the hit, the Mexicans are going to kill me! Okay, maybe he won't come out of his cell today, or maybe he got moved. Calm down!"*

"Last call!" the guard yelled.

Terrell came out of his cell and headed towards the lunch room. Terrell was standing at the end of the lunch line when he got a bump on the shoulder. It was a member of the Mexican Mafia. He gestured with his hands for Terrell to follow him.

Terrell followed him. They headed to the kitchen, where the mafia member started waving his hand. He pointed to the dish room and said, "He's in there. Hurry up. Make it quick."

Terrell followed. He was led to a room where inmates did dishes. There was usually a security guard on guard, but not today. He went in by himself while the Mexican mafia member stood guard.

Terrell spotted Trouble with his back to the door and headsets in his ear, jamming to some music.

"Here's the moment of truth: he has his back turned. It's the perfect time to strike," Terrell thought. He stood for a few seconds, hesitating, trying to figure out what to do! Whatever it was, he knew he had to do it fast before the Mexican mafia member on guard got suspicious. While Trouble's back was turned, Terrell grabbed him by the neck and put the knife to his ribs, backing him away from the dishes; he knelt, pulling Trouble with him as he talked in his ear in a firm, serious voice.

"Don't say shit. Just listen!" Terrell hissed. Trouble tried to struggle a little until he heard that. "Look, we ain't got time. I'm here to kill you, and as much as I would love to, I can't. I got to be here for my little boy. Unlike you, I'm not a killer. Look, I'm going to let you go, but don't try nothing and do nothing stupid, man. We have to get out of this mess," Terrell whispered.

Trouble nodded his head. "Okay, okay," he mumbled.

Terrell let him go from his headlock. Trouble turned around in haste. "Man, what the fuck?!" he screamed.

"Not now," said Terrell. "If the thug standing guard comes back here, then we're both dead. I made a deal with Angel to kill you,

Okay? I'll explain later. For now, I'm going to make some noises with a couple of pots and pans, and you need to lie down and act like you're stabbed, dead, or something!"

Terrell looked around for a hot sauce or ketchup, anything that could be mistaken for blood. He found something red. "Here, put this on your shirt. Hold your side like you're stabbed just in case he walks back here."

Just as planned, they caused a ruckus to make it sound like they were fighting. Now Terrell had to make it out of the dishwashing area past the man standing guard. He approached the man with the knife in his hand. "It's done," Terrell said as he handed the thug guard the knife. But just as Terrell tried to exit the room, another member of the Mexican mafia blocked him.

"Wait! It's a double cross!" the mafia member told Terrell.

Terrell threw up his hands. "Wait! Wait! I did what you wanted me to do. There's no need for this!" he said, backing away. Seeing his life flash before his eyes, all Terrell could think of was, *"How foolish of me. Foolish of me to make a deal with Angel, and now I'm going to die in jail just like Dee!"*

At that very moment, he was filled with a fit of rage. He stood firm, threw up his guard, and said, "If I go out, I'm going out with a fight."

The two men approach, one with a knife, but they both suddenly come to a halt. Their eyes widened as if they had seen a ghost. Standing behind Terrell was Trouble with a ketchup-stained shirt, standing right by the kitchen's fire alarm. He pulled down the red fire alarm switch, which triggered the alarm and sprinklers to turn on. With the alarm going off, the correctional officers were sure to be there in no time, so the Mexican mafia members fled the scene immediately.

"Don't worry. I work in the kitchen, and I got this. You have to get out of here. Go! Go!" Trouble told Terrell.

Terrell went back to his cell, shaken up from the event that just occurred. After making it back to his cell without incident, he sat on his bunk, reflecting. He realized it was only a matter of time before

Angel found out what happened and put a hit on him again. As for Trouble, he was able to fake a medical emergency and was sent to the infirmary. This was how he was able to explain why he tripped the fire alarm.

Trouble had the same thing on his mind; he knew it was only a matter of time before Angel came for both of them.

◆◆◆◆◆

After the showdown in the kitchen, Trouble, knowing that his past was catching up to him, reached out to Detective Ford, offering crucial evidence to bring closure to the case.

Detective Ford was sitting in his cubicle, slumping over his desk, fast asleep. Steam was rising from the coffee sitting in front of him. One of his fellow officers tapped him on the shoulder and said, "Hey buddy, it's been a long day. How about you go home and get some rest?"

Detective Ford rubbed his forehead and responded, "I've contacted the prosecutor and the judge's office and still haven't heard anything."

Just as Detective Ford was speaking, the phone rang. It was a call from the jail. He answered on the first ring.

"Hello, Detective Ford. You have a collect call from the Texas State Correctional Facility. To accept this call, press 8," the phone operator said.

Detective Ford pressed 8.

"Hello?" Detective Ford said.

"Hey, it's Trouble," Trouble said.

"Hello Trouble, how can I help you?" Detective Ford asked.

"You can help me by getting me and Terrell the fuck out of this facility!" He rambled on, yelling and screaming. "I almost died! Terrell tried to kill me! It was a double cross—"

"Wait, wait!" Detective Ford cut in. "slow down, slow down! Take a deep breath." He waited until he heard Trouble inhale and exhale deeply. "Okay. Are you calm?" Detective Ford asked.

"Yes," Trouble said.

"Okay, now tell me what happened," Detective Ford said.

Trouble explained everything to Detective Ford, and before he got off the phone, he told him that they were in danger and he needed to do something for their safety.

"I'm doing the best I can do. Just hang in there and stay safe. I need about two days," Detective Ford told Trouble.

"What two days?" Trouble screamed. "You don't understand. Angel and his gang run this prison! As soon as Angel finds out I'm still alive, Terrell and I are both dead!"

"Look, let me get to work. You guys watch your back the best way you can; hang in there. I'll think of something! You'll be hearing from me soon." Detective Ford hung up.

"Well, that didn't sound good," said Officer Price, who was still standing in Detective Ford's cubicle. Detective Ford looked up and said, "Don't you have some work to do?"

Officer Price held up some files and nodded. "Oh yea, you're right," he replied and walked away.

Detective Ford got back to work, making calls to the judge and sending email after email to the prosecutor's office.

At least one hour passed before Officer Price appeared again at Detective Ford's cubicle entrance.

"You again!" said Detective Ford.

"You know us police officers and detectives, we need to stick together. You know, I remember when you used to be one of us—" Officer Price said, referring to when Detective Ford was just a street-beat police officer.

"Hey, I don't have time for this! What do you want?" Detective Ford asked.

"You mentioned something about your guy being in Texas Correctional prison," Officer Price said.

"Okay, and?" Detective Ford asked curtly.

"Well, you know my partner, Chris?" Officer Price asked. Detective Ford nodded his head yes. "He was a correctional officer over there for ten years before he became a police officer. Maybe I can get him to make a few calls, maybe even get the Warden of the prison on the phone," Officer Price offered.

With excitement, Detective Ford responded, "What? You'll do that for me?"

"Just give me the word, and I'll get the investigation started," Officer Price replied.

"Investigation? Ain't no investigation. Just get me the number. Remember, you are a police officer; you leave the detective work for the detectives," Detective Ford retorted.

Officer Price gave a thumbs-up and walked away.

It was the end of a long, exhausting workday for Detective Ford, so he decided to head home for some much-needed rest.

◆◆◆◆◆

Early the next morning, Detective Ford walked into the station, grabbed his usual cup of coffee from the break room, and headed to his cubicle to start the day. As he went to sit in his chair, he noticed a sticky on his desk. He picked it up and read it. It was from Officer Price. It read: *Here's the number to the Warden at the prison you requested. PS: Not bad for a little detective work, don't you say?*

Detective Ford chuckled as he sat down in his chair to check his voicemail. To Detective Ford's surprise, it was the prosecutor's office informing him that they were aware of the newly found evidence and confession and that the judge would be reviewing the information and new findings.

"Great! That's good news!" Detective Ford said out loud.

After listening to the voicemail from the prosecutor's office, Detective Ford contacted the warden at the prison. The warden agreed to arrange for Angel and some members of his gang to be moved to a different prison facility. This way, Terrell won't be in any danger of getting a wrongful conviction overturned.

Now, as Detective Ford's relentless pursuit of justice continued, the intricate web of lies and deceit surrounding the wrongful conviction began to unravel further. With the confession of one of the true perpetrators in hand, he worked tirelessly to ensure that Terrell would be acquitted and reunited with his family after years of wrongful imprisonment.

After a long and arduous legal battle, the day finally came when the truth was officially recognized. The charges against the two wrongly accused men — Terrell and the deceased Dee — were dropped, and they were acquitted of all crimes.

Terrell's heart filled with a mix of emotions — relief, gratitude, and a burning desire to rebuild his life and reconnect with his son and mother after years of separation. Tears of relief and joy streamed down his and his mom's faces as they walked out of the courthouse.

Terrell was finally a free man once again.

Despite the efforts of Detective Ford and the authorities to bring him to justice, Bad News remained elusive, slipping through their fingers like a shadow in the night.

Bad News, knowing that his past deeds were catching up to him, harbored a deep-seated desire for revenge against Trouble and Terrell for confessing the truth, which, to him, had jeopardized his newfound freedom and peace. So, he plotted his next move. He vowed to silence the ones who had dared to expose his crimes.

Terrell, though free, was haunted by the specter of his past. He found himself caught in the crosshairs of a dangerous game of cat and mouse with Bad News. He knew that his only chance of survival as a free man lay in confronting the darkness that had followed him for so long. This darkness was Bad News.

He concluded that he might have to be the hunter and not the hunted.

As Terrell moved around town with his son, Bad News lurked in the shadows, watching, waiting.

To be continued...

Made in the USA
Coppell, TX
14 November 2024

39796185R00046